LADY IN WHITE

The Final Curtain Call

STANLEY D. LOWERY

This book is a work of fiction. Names, characters, businesses, organizations, places, and events are the product of the author's imagination and are used fictitiously. Any closeness to actual persons, living or dead, events, or locales is entirely coincidental.

For information, contact: Stan Lowery
(stanleylowery365@Gmail.com)

Book and Cover design by Stan Lowery
ISBN: 979-8-9946092-1-7

First Edition: 2026

Table of Context

Chapter 1 The Job Offer..................................1
Chapter 2 First Contact, November 17.........9
Chapter 3 December 8................................13
Chapter 4 The Red Truck............................30
Chapter 5 Bound and Desperate................53
Chapter 6 The Steel Staircase.....................64
Chapter 7 The Letter...................................80
Chapter 8 Aunt Sara...................................95
The Final Curtain Call...................................116
A Diagram of our family tree.........................119

Chapter 1

The Job Offer.

The air was filled with the sounds and scent of food vendors preparing popcorn and cotton candy for the day's big event. Intense rays of the summer sun were making heat waves shimmer just above the black pavement of Main Street. My crew and I had just spent three grueling hours setting the stage and audio for a street festival. This was my first day back to work since my mother passed just a week ago in a tragic car accident.

The headliner was an R&B band that peaked in 1977, riding the wave of success from four big hits that year. As I wiped the sweat from my brow, I noticed a distinguished dark-haired man with a silvering mustache and beard approaching from my left side. His jacket collar was clinched between his finger and his thumb and slung over his shoulder. His shirt sleeves were rolled to his forearms to beat the day's heat. In August of 2009, the heat wave was almost unbearable. He pulls on his tie and loosens it,

"Hi, are you David Foley?"

"Yes, David Braxton Foley, my friends call me DB, but I'm a little busy right now."

"My name is Bill. Do you have a minute to talk?"

"I'd like to, Bill, but we're just starting sound check. Can it wait until later in the week?"

"Oh no, we need you now. It will only take a few minutes. I want to offer you a new job, a job as Production Director at a brand-new theatre in town."

I remained with full attention to the soundboard in front of me, the band on stage, and the sweltering heat relentlessly beating down on us.

"I have asked around, and everyone says you are just what we need at the theatre."

Finally, I looked up and made eye contact with Bill. His eyes were empty and dark, lacking sleep, with dark circles beneath them.

"I'm not sure who you talked to, but I have a job."

"If you will give me five minutes of your time, I'm sure I can make it worth your while."

I knew this man was not going away.

"Give me fifteen minutes to finish sound check, and we can talk." This seemed to satisfy him, then he pointed to a shaded area on the court square.

"I'll meet you over there in fifteen minutes."

As he walked away, I shook my head in disbelief and returned my attention to the sound check I was knee-deep into.

I finished sound check and looked forward to a short break and a cool drink. I hit the ice chest, grabbed an ice-cold bottle of water, and headed across the street.

The shade of the large oak trees was cool. Bill did indeed offer me a job, one that I felt I had been training for most of my life. This job would be a great opportunity and challenge, both a good distraction from the last few weeks.

"If you would stop by the theatre tomorrow, I will introduce you to Sam, my business partner and co-owner. "

The next day, after finishing my morning coffee at Lily Bean's, I walked two blocks to the theatre. As I neared the grand entrance of the Marquee, an unexpected shiver coursed through me, evoking a peculiar sense of familiarity, as though I had crossed this threshold countless times. Pulling the heavy door outward, I felt a refreshing coolness embrace me. As I made my way into the lobby, Bill extended a welcoming hand, his grip firm.

"So pleased you could join us today. Come, allow me to introduce you to my associate, Sam."

As we walked to their huge office, it felt almost like a homecoming. Surrounded by antique, timeworn furnishings, a subtle, unsettling atmosphere began to take hold. Sam's office door was slightly open, and we entered.

"Sam, this is the individual I mentioned yesterday. This is David Foley. His friends call him DB."

Without even raising his gaze, Sam's voice, laced with irritation, boomed, "Indeed, indeed. David Foley, I guess you will be tasked with managing all contractual agreements and artist riders for our upcoming engagements. Bill, escort him to his backstage workspace."

Our departure was silent and wordless. As we retraced our steps through the lobby, Bill leaned in toward me, his voice a low murmur,

“Pay him no mind. He’s currently carrying a significant burden. He’ll warm up to you in due time.” Bill briefly showed me around as we made our way backstage.

The office I would occupy was not grand by any measure. It was located just off the stage entrance and was convenient and close to the action during productions. I knew I would be spending numerous days and long evenings working from that office. Once again, I felt a sense of belonging, a connection I can’t explain.

The theatre was built in 1939 and started out as a movie house. There was a grand Art Deco facade entrance and beautiful curved walls inside the lobby. In the main theatre, burgundy drapes formed a warm frame around a beautiful mahogany floored stage. In that moment, I thought about the old movies of the golden era playing on the silver screen just feet away from my office. As a kid,

I lived a couple of blocks from the old Majestic theatre. My older brothers would tell me that it was haunted and tell ghost stories late at night.

Bill interrupted my daydreaming and asked,

"Well, DB, can you start right away?"

"Of course, I'll be here bright and early tomorrow morning."

The next day, when I arrived, I was greeted with my name on my office door and an eighteen-inch-high stack of paperwork on my desk. I could see that these contracts and riders had been accumulating for weeks, and I understood Bill's appearance the day we met. I dove into the pile and started sorting by date.

I knew this was not going to be an easy task and would take multiple days to clear. The days turned into weeks, and it didn't seem like I was making headway. I was two weeks into the stack, and I was down to my last two contracts. I was determined to finish, so I pressed on. The night grew long.

This late-night work session would prove to be a little different. I began to hear noises; I wrote them off as the old building settling or the wind blowing the doors. I said jokingly,

"If you are a spirit, you need to show yourself." I never heard anyone speak back to me, thank God, but a dark theatre and creaking noises can play tricks on your eyes and other senses.

Chapter 2

First Contact, November 17

November brings cool, brisk mornings in the foothills of North Carolina. As I walked from the coffee shop to the backstage entrance, I flipped my collar up to block the cold air against my neck and ears. The back entrance was my norm each morning, as my office was only a few feet inside. I settled in and began working on contracts for artists who would play the theatre in the coming months. It must have been around 8 am. For the next 6 hours, I studied each contract intensely. My eyes grew weary, so I was about to make my fifth cup of coffee. I leaned back in my chair and raised my arms high over my head with a big stretch and a yawn.

From a distance, soft music began to play, and a sweet smell of perfume began to fill my small, cluttered office. It was a hauntingly familiar smell; my mother wore something similar.

I turned quickly to the door, expecting to greet a visitor, but no one was there. Leaning my head hard to the right, I could see up the hall a few feet, my eyes squinting to see in the dim light, but nothing was there. As quickly as the soft music and sweet smell filled my office, it began to dissipate. My mind was racing; I tried to continue working on the contracts, but my sight was blurring. My eyes were tired, and my back and legs ached from hours of sitting. I rubbed my eyes and leaned back once again for a stretch.

When I sat forward, the contract I was working on had changed. What was before me now was a contract dated September 13, 1961. The artist was one I had never heard of before, “Lily White.” I glanced at the agreed-upon price, $300.00. This was nothing compared to what we pay most artists today. As I read further into the contract, the soft music and the perfume scent returned.

This time, I was really shaken. I jumped up and stuck my head out the door, knowing I would see someone from the front office there, maybe playing a joke on me, but there was no one.

I walked, okay, I practically ran to the front office to see if either Bill or Sam was joking around. They were both working away as if nothing weird were going on. I interrupted their busy work,

"Hey, guys, do either of you know anything about an old contract that got mixed in with the batch on my desk this morning?"

Sam replied,

"The only contracts you should have are for new shows coming up, not past shows."

As I turn around to return to my office, Bill speaks up,

"There is an old file box in the storage room with old contracts, some old show bills, and newspapers in it. One may have gotten mixed in with yours somehow, but we haven't been in there in months."

Sam cut his eyes at Bill, disapproving of his statement.

"Just get back to work and do your job."

When I returned to my office, I sat down at my desk only to discover the contract I had been working on was back where it had started. The 1961 contract was nowhere to be found. The music and smell of sweet perfume were gone, and no hint of them lingered.

I figured I would see or hear something extraordinary over the next few days, but nothing, no music, no perfume, no noises, nothing. Three weeks passed. I often thought of the old contract. Was I dreaming or hallucinating?

Chapter 3

December 8.

The days are shorter. A cold rain was falling, and no amount of coffee could have offset the morning chill. The vigorous walk from the coffee shop was filled with puddled obstacles and curbside splashes from passing automobiles.

I eventually made my way to the now-familiar stage entrance. I hurried inside to my cramped office. I tossed my umbrella in the corner and looked down at my pant legs, which were drenched. The small space heater under my desk feels warm on my legs, and before long, my trousers are dry. I found a new set of contracts on my desk. A note marked urgent in Sam's scribbled handwriting stuck to the top one.

I began scanning through the contract. Before getting too far into the rider portion, I again begin to hear soft music and smell the now unforgettable perfume. This time, I hear voices: a man and woman are arguing. It is coming from the stage.

"William, I am sorry, I am heartbroken from the decision we were forced to make a year ago."

"Lily, this will destroy everything we have worked for. If people find out, I will be ruined."

I jumped up and rushed to the stage door as I peered onto the dark stage. I saw the white glow of a woman's gown move from stage left to stage right. I stood frozen, my heart pounding in my chest. The arguing voices had stopped, the lady in white was gone, and the stage was now silent and dark. I couldn't make out any figures; my whole body shivered as if someone had walked over my grave.

Retreating to my office, I closed the door, my hands shaking. I tried to rationalize what I had seen, smelled, and heard. Nothing made sense.

This time, the sweet perfume lingered, and I found myself wondering about the lady in the white gown. Who was Lily? Could this be the same Lily mentioned in the old contract?

With each new live performance at the theatre, I found myself obsessed with uncovering its hidden history. I delved into old records, looking for any mention of the mysterious artist in the 1961 contract. It was as if this place held secrets it didn't want to be revealed.

One evening, after everyone had left, I decided to explore the storage room Bill had mentioned. I located several old file boxes covered in dust and cobwebs. As I opened the first of them, the scent of the perfume wafted up, and I knew I was on the right track.

Inside were stacks of yellowing contracts and playbills. I carefully sorted through them, discovering a treasure trove of the theatre's past.

It was then that I realized I might have found her: a performer named Lily White, famed for her beauty and grace. The playbill featured a beautiful singer wearing a white stage gown. It was attached to a contract dated 1961, and the agreed-upon price was $300. I felt a shiver as I realized I might have found the spirit haunting the stage just outside my office. But why was she still here, and what did she want?

I continued my clandestine investigations. In the old storage room Bill had mentioned, I discovered a newspaper article. The headlines read " Singer Falls To Her Death During Rehearsal." The article went on to say how Lily had been a rising star, performing at the theatre during its heyday. She had captivated audiences with her ethereal presence and haunting vocals. The tragedy was ruled an accident that night, her life cut short in the very theatre that had once celebrated her talent.

As I delved deeper into the theatre's past, I discovered that Lily's death had been ruled an accident; however, the actual cause of her fall had never been determined. It seemed to me that the theatre's management at the time, eager to protect its reputation, had swept the incident under the rug.

But why was Lily still lingering here, her spirit unable to move on? Was it because her death had been unjustly forgotten, or was there something more she needed to reveal? I became determined to uncover the truth and give her the justice she deserved. I spent countless nights in the storage room, poring over old records and playbills, searching for any clues that might lead me to the answers I sought.

One night, as I was working late in my office, I again heard the voices arguing from the stage. I froze.

"Is that Lily?"

I crept near the stage door, their figures were illuminated by a single spotlight as I watched, hidden in the shadows.

"William, when you walked away a year ago, you left me no choice. I did what I did, and now we must live with the consequences. I have moved on, and I suggest you do the same."

She pushed away from him. He grabbed her arm. They struggled. She fell, hitting her head on the mahogany stage floor. As I stood there, shocked and horrified, Lily's face pale and lifeless, her eyes opened, looking directly at me. Her eyes filled with sorrow and distress, as if pleading with me to understand. At that moment, I knew Lily White and the spirit were the same.

After that night, Lily's spirit was quiet. I was not sure I would ever hear from her again. It was as if, by bearing witness to the truth of her death, I had finally set her spirit free. The theatre, however, seemed to emit a hint of her presence, a lingering echo of her tragic story, maybe only in my mind.

I often found myself thinking of her, remembering the lessons I had learned about the power of truth and the enduring nature of love and passion. The theatre, with all its secrets and mysteries, had become a place of reflection and inspiration, a reminder that the past is always with us, wanting to be remembered or waiting to be uncovered and understood.

New performers graced our stage over the next few weeks. I thought about the theatre's hidden history and Lily's tragic tale. I often found myself wandering the empty corridors, imagining the bustling atmosphere of its heyday. The faint scent of the sweet perfume lingered, a constant reminder of the mystery surrounding Lily White.

My curiosity got the better of me, and I began digging deeper into the old records and newspapers in the storage room. I uncovered more details about her life and career. She had been a rising star, her name synonymous with elegance and talent. But it was her tragic death that seemed to be the theatre's best-kept secret. I began to feel a sense of responsibility to uncover the truth and ensure her story was not forgotten.

"I wonder if any of the stagehands or performers from that time are still around now?"

I looked at every playbill and old contract I could find. One name kept surfacing, Margaret London. She performed on some of the same shows as Lily. I began looking online for entertainers with the last name London. I hit a dead end. The next morning, I arrived at the theatre early. I caught Bill as he was pulling into his parking spot.

"Hey Bill, you got a minute?"

"Sure, let's get inside out of the cold."

When we walked into his office, Sam was already there.

Bill said, "What can I do for you?"

"I was looking at some of the old contracts and was interested in some of the old artists back in the day."

Sam looked up, "Mr. Foley, we don't pay you to look at old contracts; we pay you to address the new ones. Leave those old contracts alone and take care of your work."

I turned to leave, and Bill put his hand on my shoulder and walked out with me.

"I was just curious about a few names. I was not neglecting my work."

Bill said in a whisper, "What names? Maybe I can help."

"At this point, just one name, Margaret London. I know she performed with Lily White on occasion, but I can't seem to find anything about her today. Do you think she is still around?"

Bill stopped in his tracks. His eyebrows rose, and he looked away from me.

"No, I don't think I have heard that name before. I need to get back to work, and you do the same."

Bill turned abruptly and headed back toward his office.

A few days later, as I sat in my office sipping coffee, thinking about how Bill reacted when I mentioned Margaret. A soft knock on my door startled me. I opened the door to find an elderly woman standing there.

"Hello, my name is Margaret. I used to perform here years ago."

My eyes lit up with surprise. I said,

"Margaret London?"

With a smile, she replied,

"That was my stage name. I heard you've been looking into the history of the theatre," her eyes sparkling with a mixture of curiosity and wariness. I invited her in, and over a cup of tea, she shared stories of the theatre's glory days. She spoke of Lily with a fond smile, remembering her talent and beauty.

As our hot tea cooled in our cups, Margaret's stories painted a vivid picture of the past. I learned about the vibrant community that had once filled these halls and the artists who had graced the stage, but she revealed none of the secrets kept within these walls.

“Do you remember the night Lily White died? Were you here?”

Margaret's face clouded over.

"It was a tragedy," she said softly. "Some say an argument, a lovers' quarrel. But the truth is, she tripped on her long white gown, fell, and hit her head. It was simply an accident.”

Her voice was laced with certainty.

“As you grow older, you will understand that theatres are not just buildings; they hold the memories and spirits of all who have performed and watched within their walls. I can imagine Lily's spirit may still linger, not because she has a tragic story to tell but because she misunderstood compliments as affection. The story does not deserve your attention. Take my advice and leave it alone." With that, Margaret rose to leave.

"Thank you for your time and stories, Mrs. London." As she was leaving, she glanced onto the stage; her gaze lingered only a second or two. I'm not sure how Margaret fits into this puzzle, but she does know more than she is telling me.

I did not take her advice, and I felt a renewed sense of purpose. I felt an even greater connection to the theatre's past, knowing that the mysteries it held were slowly unraveling. As I looked more closely at the theatre's history, I became intrigued by Margaret's presence in this mysterious puzzle. I wanted to know more about this woman who had witnessed both the theatre's glory days and the lowest point of its hidden history.

With this new lead, I continued my research, eager to uncover more of the connection between Margaret and Lily. According to an old newspaper clipping I found, Margaret and Lily had been close friends and rising stars on the theatre stage. They had often performed together, captivating audiences with their stunning shows.

However, Lily's death casts a dark shadow over Margaret's life. A small article in one newspaper read, Margaret London's wedding postponed due to the tragic death of her best friend. I wondered if the trauma of losing her friend had really caused the postponement.

I searched for more information about Margaret's wedding, curious to learn whether she had eventually married and what path her life had taken. But the files offered no further details, leaving me with more questions than answers.

I continued my investigations, trying to piece together the fragments of the theatre's past like a complex jigsaw puzzle. I felt a strong need to uncover the truth and honor Lily's legacy and memories.

The scent of the sweet perfume lingered faintly, a constant reminder of Lily's presence and the secrets that still awaited discovery. My curiosity about the theatre's history and Lily's spirit only deepened as I delved into the Majestic's mysterious past.

I spent many late nights in the storage room, carefully examining the old file boxes Bill had mentioned. Just as I would think there were no more boxes, I would find another. The sixty years of files, contracts, and newspapers seem endless.

Among the yellowing contracts and playbills, I came across another newspaper clipping. The headlines revealed a shocking twist to the story. “THEATRE OWNERSHIP CHANGES HANDS.” Just four years after Lily's tragic death. Further research uncovered a hidden scandal. It seemed that Lily's family had filed a wrongful death lawsuit against the theatre, claiming negligence and demanding compensation for their loss. The theatre eventually filed for bankruptcy and faced financial ruin. Then, unexpectedly, in

1965, a buyer emerged and purchased the property for a fraction of its value. After that date, the lawsuit seems to have disappeared, with no further mention of it or the theatre.

I felt a chill as I realized the extent of the theatre's secrets and the lengths people would go to in order to protect their interests. I couldn't shake the feeling that there was more to uncover, and I became determined to find out who had orchestrated the lawsuit's disappearance and why.

I spent the next few weeks reaching out to local historians and legal experts, trying to piece together the puzzle. It was a challenging task, as many records from that era were incomplete or lost over the years. However, my persistence paid off when I discovered a connection between the new owner and a prominent law firm in the city. It seemed the buyer had ties to the legal world, and I began to suspect the lawsuit's disappearance might not have been a coincidence.

After weeks of research and uncovering more pieces of the theatre's hidden history, I felt closer to the truth, but my investigation into Margaret revealed another surprising twist. I discovered that she had retired from acting shortly after Lily's death, but, interestingly, had done very well financially.

I spent a day at the public records office, pretending to research for a paper, and uncovered tax records showing that Margaret received substantial annual payments from a local law firm. This discovery left me with more questions than answers. Was Margaret somehow involved in the disappearance of the wrongful death lawsuit against the theatre? And if so, what role did she play in all of this?

I decided to visit Margaret, this time with more pointed questions. I wanted to understand her relationship with Lily and the theatre, and why she had chosen to leave the acting world behind.

As I approached her home, I felt a sense of anticipation and unease. When Margaret answered the door, she greeted me with a cautious smile.

“Hello, what are you doing here?”

“Our last conversation intrigued me, and I wondered if we could talk further?”

“Of course, come in, we can talk in the den.”

The small room was decorated with old photos of her past, including one of her and Lily performing on stage. I could sense her wariness as I probed deeper into her past. She shared memories of her time at the theatre, her friendship with Lily, and the trauma of losing her dear friend. But when I asked about the lawsuit and her unexpected retirement, Margaret's demeanor changed. She became guarded, her eyes darting away as if searching for an escape.

"I did what I had to do to move on," her soft voice laced with a mixture of sadness and determination. "Sometimes, we make choices to protect ourselves and those we care about." Her words were hollow and insincere, leaving me to wonder if she was hinting at something more.

"I love the pictures of you and Lily, but I don't see any of your husband, William."

Margarete's eyes filled with tears, "William and I never married. He passed a few years after Lily. I loved him so, but it was not meant to be."

Stunned and at a loss for words, I thanked Margaret for her time and turned to leave. I felt a sense of unease settle over me. I couldn't shake the feeling that Margaret had more secrets than just the night Lily passed.

The pieces of the puzzle were there, but they didn't quite fit together. I needed to find another angle, another source of information, to fully understand the extent of the theatre's secrets and Margaret's role in them. Little did I know that my search for answers would lead me down an even more unexpected path, one that would forever change my understanding of the theatre's history and the spirit that haunted its halls.

Chapter 4

The Red Truck.

The next morning, while sitting at a window booth at the coffee shop just down the street from the theatre. I began to think, was there something more sinister involved between Lily, her lover, Margaret, and this law firm? Or is it just a coincidence that put these particular people together?

As I walked to the theatre from the coffee shop, I crossed the street as the light changed. From out of nowhere, a truck swerved and missed me by only inches in the crosswalk. I dove to safety. I rolled into the grass and turned to try and get the tag number, but they sped off in a cloud of grey exhaust.

I brushed myself off and made my way toward the theatre. As I approached, a sense of unease crept over me. I noticed a figure turn the corner. My curiosity heightened, I quickened my pace to catch a glimpse. To my surprise, I saw the same red truck that had swerved at me earlier. My heart raced. Is there a connection between these incidents? Was someone deliberately trying to harm me? I felt a chill as I realized the potential danger I was in.

Retreating to the safety of the theatre, I entered through the stage door, my mind racing with questions. I decided to confide in Bill, sharing the strange occurrences of the past few days. I walked straight to Bill's office. Sam was at his desk reading a newspaper, so I got Bill's attention and motioned to him to come out into the lobby. I told him of the red truck and other things that had happened. With a concerned look, Bill said,

"Let's take a look at the security footage to try and identify the truck or maybe its driver."

"Do we have cameras around the theatre?"

"Yes, two outside cameras and one in the ticket booth. They are in this closet behind the display cabinets."

As we scrutinized the grainy images, we discovered the truck had been circling the block before my encounter in the crosswalk. It was clear that someone was deliberately targeting me, but why? The following days were marked by heightened vigilance. I found myself constantly looking over my shoulder, wondering if the truck would appear again.

I returned to my office, and once again the sweet smell of Lavender & Rose filled the air. I heard faint voices coming from the stage. My heart pounded as I recognized Lily's voice, and I knew she was trying to communicate something. Once again, Lily and William were arguing about the choice she had made. She turned to walk away, and William grabbed her arm. Lily pulled away just before she fell and hit the stage floor. I wanted to help, I needed to help, but I didn't know how or what to do. I felt compelled to uncover the truth behind her tragic death and the secrets this theatre held. The mystery of Lily's spirit and the theatre's hidden history filled my thoughts.

I decided to confront Bill and Sam to see if they had any information. With determination, I approached their shared office and found them both immersed in their work.

"Hey, guys," trying to sound casual. "I wanted to touch base with you about something odd that's been happening lately." I briefly explained the strange occurrences, including the old contract, the perfume scent, and the argument I had witnessed on stage. I watched their reactions carefully, searching for any signs of guilt or surprise.

Sam, always the more talkative one, leaned back in his chair and rubbed his chin.

"Wow, that's quite a story, Foley. I mean, we've all heard stories about this place being haunted, but I never thought much of it."

He exchanged a glance with Bill, who remained silent, his eyes narrowed in thought. With a look of contempt on his face, Sam says,

"I suppose Lily's spirit may be trying to communicate with you. Have you considered doing some research on her?"

I nodded, feeling a mix of relief and frustration. "I've been trying to dig up information, but it's like this place is determined to keep its secrets buried. I can't help but wonder if there's something more to uncover." I paused, then added, "Have either of you come across anything unusual in your time here? Any stories or incidents that might be relevant?"

Bill, usually reserved, spoke up.

"I can't say I have. This theatre has its fair share of ghost stories, but nothing concrete. Though now that you mention it, I do recall hearing something about a performer from long ago who met an untimely end, but that was long before our time. Good luck finding anyone who's been around longer than us."

The suggestion resonated, and I made a mental note to explore that lead.

As I turned to leave, Sam called out,

"Be careful, though, Mr. Foley. Sometimes, digging up the past can unleash things we're not prepared for."

His words sent a shiver through my entire body, and I wondered if this was truly a word of caution or a threat in some way.

I returned to my office, my mind raced with questions and theories. I couldn't focus on my work, constantly questioning the role of Sam and Bill, two individuals I hadn't previously suspected. I felt a sense of urgency to unravel the mystery, but also a growing sense of caution. The theatre seemed to be guarding its secrets closely, and I wondered if I was getting too close to the truth. I know that my quest for answers could lead me down a path of the unexpected. Forever changing my perception of this place and the spirits that dwelled within its walls.

Bill and Sam's suggestion to find someone who had been around longer than they had only fueled my determination. Hesitantly, I started a file on them. Curious about their knowledge of the building's secrets and their potential connection to the strange occurrences. I delved into old records, searching for any mention of them or their families.

As it turned out, the theatre held its secrets tightly, but I did discover that both their families had deep roots in the city and that their grandparents had been patrons of the theatre since its early days. But nothing indicated their awareness of the truth behind Lily's death or the theatre's hidden scandals.

As I continued my clandestine investigations, I felt a growing sense of unease. The sweet perfume of Lily's presence lingered, and I often found myself glancing over my shoulder, wondering if she was trying to warn me of something.

The more I uncovered, the more I felt like someone was watching me, perhaps even following me. I began to question if my curiosity had put me in danger. Yet, I couldn't shake the feeling that I was onto something, and the thought of uncovering the truth kept me going.

One late night, as I was leaving the theatre after another fruitless search, I noticed a figure standing in the shadows across the street. I took a deep breath, and I recognized the silhouette of the red truck that had almost hit me before. I quickly turned and started to hurry back into the theatre, my mind racing with questions. Were they watching me? And if so, who were they and what did they want?

The hair on my neck stood on end as I thought about the theatre's secrets and the danger that came along with those secrets. My curiosity about the figure across the street and their connection to the red truck was overwhelming. I took another deep breath and decided to confront them. I stepped out of the doorway and into the street light.

As I approached, the figure melted back into the darkness, retreating into an alleyway. I followed, my heart pounding, and called out,

"Who are you? Why are you following me?" There was no response, only the faint sound of footsteps retreating further into the alley. I quickened my pace, determined to get answers.

As I turned the corner, a hand grabbed my shoulder, and I spun around to find myself face-to-face with Bill.

"What are you doing?" his eyes searched mine.

"I saw you following that person. Be careful, they could be dangerous."

I realized then that Bill knew something. "What aren't you telling me?" I demanded. "You and Sam seem to know more about this place and its secrets than you let on. Why are you keeping things from me?"

Bill hesitated, his gaze flicking to the ground. "It's complicated," he murmured. "There are things about this theatre that we don't fully understand. We've experienced strange occurrences and uncovered hidden scandals, but we've never probed too deeply. It seems that you've stumbled upon something that someone wants to keep hidden, and they're willing to go to great lengths to protect their secrets."

As I turned, Bill grabbed my arm, pulling me close. His breath was hot in my ear as he whispered,

"I know more than I can or should say. I'm just as afraid as you are. I, too, have had close calls, and they accomplished what they aimed to do." His eyes, filled with a mix of fear and determination, held mine for a moment. "Meet me at the coffee shop in the morning. There are too many ears at the theatre." With that, he slowly turned, walked away, and disappeared into the shadows.

The next morning, I arrived at the coffee shop early, my heart pounding with anticipation. Chad, the barista, took my order and leaned in close.

"So, what's going on at the theatre this morning?" his eyes sparkling with curiosity.

It gave me chills as images of Lily flashed through my mind. At that moment, I knew Bill would not be joining me.

Simultaneously, crimson strobes pulsed in the windowpane as the emergency vehicles converged on the theatre. My coffee crashed to the floor; I bolted through the back exit, a frantic dash covering the entire distance to the theatre. Rounding the final corner, I witnessed the infamous red pickup truck disappearing down the street. I was paralyzed, my pulse a frantic drum.

What unspeakable act had they committed? Could they be connected to Bill's no-show at the coffee shop? The truck's hasty retreat only deepened the mystery. I was left standing there, alone, the morning sunlight revealing nothing but an empty street.

The police were exiting their cars and beginning to enter the building. Several headed around the side of the theatre to the rear, and one officer spotted me. He cautiously approached me with a tactical L position. With a harsh commanding voice,

"Stop where you are and get on the ground. We have a situation, and for your safety and ours, don't move."

He approached cautiously and placed handcuffs on me.

"You are only detained and not under arrest. What business do you have at the theatre, and why were you running toward the theatre?"

"I work here and saw the red lights headed here and wanted to see what was happening."

I dared not mention that I had a vision of Lily in white gliding across the stage, for fear that one of my employers might be in danger. He would think I was losing my mind. As I stood there, handcuffed and confused, I watched the police officers swarm the theatre, wearing tactical gear and weapons drawn. Their cautious movements and urgent demeanor indicated that a serious situation was unfolding. I felt a surge of concern for my colleagues, Bill and Sam, hoping they were safe and unaware of the looming danger. The officer who detained me, according to his badge, was Officer Davis, who held a tight grip on my arm as he led me away from the theatre.

I explained, "I am the Production Director at the theatre, and I'm worried about the safety of my colleagues."

He listened intently, his eyes narrowing with suspicion.

"We received an anonymous call about a murder at the theatre. We're taking every precaution, and your cooperation is essential."

"A murder? Is it Bill?"

His words shook me to the core as I realized the gravity of the situation. He guided me to his nearby police cruiser,

"Remain inside until the situation is under control."

My mind raced with questions and fears as I watched the officers continue their operation. I wondered if my vision of Lily and the mysterious figure in the red truck were connected to this unfolding event. Was someone targeting the theatre, and if so, why? The minutes dragged by like hours as I waited anxiously for any sign of resolution.

After what seemed like an eternity, a tall, heavy gentleman in a dark grey suit opened the door to the cruiser.

"I'm Detective Johnson. What is your business at the theatre?

"I have explained everything to Officer Davis."

His voice was gruff but steady, "Now tell me, from the beginning."

After recounting the same information I had given Davis. He opens the patrol car door further,

"Come with me inside."

As we entered the theatre, the familiar scent of the sweet perfume hit me. Detective Johnson noticed my reaction and said,

"Do you recognize the fragrance?"

I nodded, "Yes, and somehow it was connected to the ghostly presence I had encountered." He seemed intrigued but remained focused on the task at hand.

We made our way to the office that Bill and Sam shared. The door was ajar, and I felt a chill as I realized something was amiss. I think he wanted to witness my reaction as we entered. With a sense of dread, we stepped inside. As I moved around in the office, the chill deepened. The room was empty, but it felt as if a presence lingered. Detective Johnson must have sensed it as well. He paused, his eyes scanning the room.

"Do you feel that?" his voice was low. "It's almost as if someone is here, watching us."

I nodded, my heart pounding. Suddenly, I felt a rush of cold air, and the scent of the perfume became stronger.

"She's here," I whispered. "Lily White. The ghost I told you about."

The detective's eyes widened, and he reached for his gun. With a nervous smile playing at the corners of my mouth, I tried to swallow the lump in my throat.

"You don't believe in ghosts, do you, Detective?"

He shook his head, his grip on his weapon tightening.

"No, sir. I don't. But I've learned to keep an open mind."

We moved further into the room, our eyes scanning for any signs of disturbance. My gaze fell on the desk, and I noticed a stack of papers askew as if someone had been hastily searching for something. I stepped forward, drawing attention to the top sheet. It was a contract, dated September 13, 1961. My heart stopped as I realized it was the same contract I had seen before, the one that had drawn me into this mystery.

"This is it," my voice shaking. "The playbill and contract, it's how I first became aware of Lily White."

Detective Johnson took the paper from the desk, his eyes scanning the document.

"Interesting," he murmured. "And just how did you come across this contract?

“It appeared on my deck one evening while at work.”

He rolls his eyes in disbelief,

“You say this contract just appeared on your desk one day?"

I nodded, my eyes never leaving his face.

"And you've had no explanation for how it got there?"

I shook my head. "None. I thought it may be a message from Lily, a way to get my attention."

The detective's brow raised, and he placed the contract on the desk. "Well, you may be right, or you may be a little deranged. But one thing is clear, someone doesn't want you digging into the past."

As we stood there, the perfume's scent began to fade, and the chill in the room lessened. Whatever presence had been there was retreating, leaving us with more mysteries to unravel. Detective Johnson turned to me, his face stern and brow furrowed, as he gazed around the room.

"We'll get to the bottom of this, Ms. White. Mark my words. We will uncover the secrets hidden here."

As we left the office and entered the theatre lobby, the detective uncuffed me and said,

"I guess there is no reason to hold you any longer."

I felt a mix of relief and lingering unease. He handed me his card and said,

“Call me if you notice anything suspicious in the coming days.”

I watched as he and the other officers exited through the front, their absence leaving an eerie silence in their wake.

It was then that I heard a sound backstage, and I made my way toward it. I found Sam, his face etched with concern, entering from the stage door.

"Who were those men, and what did they want?" His eyes were darting between the departing officers and me.

"Where have you been? The police got an anonymous call this morning warning of... something suspicious at the theatre." I hesitated, not saying anything about murder. Sam's absence piqued my curiosity during this commotion.

His face seemed relieved with the officers' leaving, and he shook his head as if clearing away the remnants of a troubling thought.

"I was here early this morning, but when I heard about the suspicious activity, I decided to lie low. It seems I made the right choice."

The day's events had left me shaken, and I felt a pressing need to unravel the mysteries that seemed to deepen with each discovery. Sam's absence added another layer of mystery, and I grew concerned for Bill, who had failed to meet me at the coffee shop as planned. I instantly pulled my phone out of my pocket to call Bill. It went straight to voicemail. Panic-stricken, I hit redial with the same results. Frantically, I began searching the theatre for Bill, hoping to find him safe and uncover the truth behind the day's events. Strangely, Sam did not seem concerned.

“Bill does this occasionally; he disappears for days at a time, and he will turn up eventually.”

As I retraced our steps, I felt fear, half-expecting to find Bill in danger or uncover more clues about his whereabouts. The sweet perfume of Lily's presence lingered in the air, a constant reminder of the mysteries awaiting discovery. My heart pounded with anticipation as we stepped backstage, ready to confront whatever mystery the theatre held.

As Sam and I exchanged glances, I knew we both knew some of the secrets this theatre held, but I was growing increasingly suspicious that Sam was far more involved than he'd led me to believe.

“Did you see Bill at all last night? Did he say he was going anywhere today? Did you see him this morning at any time?”

“What’s with the twenty questions?” Sam's eyes narrowed, and his brow began to bead with small pearls of sweat. "You think I'm involved in

Bill's disappearance?", his voice stern and deliberate.

I detected a hint of defensiveness in his actions.

"I assure you, I had no idea Bill was to meet you at the coffee shop this morning. Bill and I may own this theatre together, but we don't share everything. He's always been a bit more... secretive about certain matters."

I studied his face, searching for any signs of deception.

"Then help me find him. We need to uncover the truth, and I believe you know more than you're letting on."

Sam hesitated, his gaze flicking between me and the stage.

"I may have an idea where he is," he conceded.

"But it's just a hunch. Bill mentioned something about an old storage unit he used to store some of his personal items. It might be a good place to start."

I said, “Okay, let’s go. Do we need to drive or walk?”

“It’s a short walk,” Sam said. “Follow me.”

We headed out the back and made our way to the storage unit, located in an unmarked building two blocks South of the theatre. As we entered the side door, the musty smell of old belongings and forgotten memories greeted us.

Sam led the way, his steps hesitant as if he, too, sensed the weight of the secrets this place might hold. We found a door slightly ajar, a faint light spilling out into the dim hallway. With a sense of trepidation, we stepped inside. The beam of our flashlights cut through the darkness, illuminating a space filled with boxes and covered furniture.

My mind is a whirlwind of emotion. As we enter the dark interior of the warehouse, I whisper,

"If you haven't seen Bill this morning, how did you know about the suspicious activity called in to the police station this morning?" My heart raced as I imagined Bill, huddled in a corner, held captive or worse.

"And how did you know Bill was going to meet me at the coffee shop this morning?"

My eyes began to adjust to the dimly lit room, as dust particles danced in the beams of light slicing through the darkness. On a table in the corner, I spot a stack of old playbills, their faded pages taunting me with secrets I knew they held. I approached the pile, my breath quickening as I realized the top program featured Lily White. I feel my heart skip a beat as I realize it was the same playbill for the night of her death.

"Sam," I whispered, my voice hoarse, "Look at this." Sam didn't answer. I strained my ears, hoping to hear some indication of his whereabouts, but only silence greeted me.

I leaned closer, my eyes widening as I recognized the significance.

"This was the night," I whispered, my voice cracked with tension. As I reached for the program, my heart hammered in my chest. Before my fingertips touched the playbill, I heard the door creak, and I felt a sudden rush of cool air. The playbill flew from the table, revealing the contract underneath. My flashlight flickered and died, plunging me into darkness. I was paralyzed, my mind racing with fear and uncertainty.

"But why would Bill have this?"

I stood there isolated and vulnerable, the musty air thick with anxiety, and I felt the coldness surround my body. Sam's absence from the storage unit was unnerving, and my mind raced with questions.

I called out to him,

“Sam, are you still here?” My voice echoed in the confined space. With no response, I was alone, bound by the shadows and the secrets that lingered in this dark place. Without warning, a sudden impact to the back of my head, I fall to my knees, my eyes dimming to total darkness

Chapter 5

Bound & Desperate

I woke, disoriented and confused, my body aching from the cold, hard floor beneath me. The realization of my captivity sank in as I felt the tight restraints on my wrists and ankles. My mind raced from the storage unit to Lily White and the figure in the red truck. Were they behind this? Had they taken Bill as well? The questions swirled in my mind as panic began to set in.

Bound and desperate, I wrestled against my restraints, and my heart rate increased. The door creaked inward. A soft angelic voice broke the silence. The smell of musk filled the air. A figure materialized in the gloom, the presence a stark contrast to the obscurity of darkness. My vision, blurred by tears from the assault, I struggled to define the shadowy form. Yet, even through the haze, a celestial grace emanated from the silhouette, with features etched with profound empathy. Swiftly, moved to my side, the bonds that held me captive began to loosen.

"Thank God, you are alive. I feared the worst when I saw you didn't come out with the other gentleman."

I sat up, rubbing my sore wrists and head as I struggled to my feet.

"What happened? Who hit me?" My voice was laced with urgency.

"Thank you for finding me, but who are you, and how did you get here?"

"Lily sent me. She sensed you were in trouble."

The throbbing in my head was immense. I slowly turned to say thank you, but no one was there. Was it an allusion to a dream, or was it a figment of my imagination?

I left the abandoned storage unit, my legs shaky and unsteady beneath me. The sunlight was harsh and bright, my eyes slowly adjusted as I emerged, and I took a moment to gather my bearings. With a cough clearing the dust from my throat, "I need to get back to the theatre." My voice was steady despite the turmoil within. "Whoever is behind this is still out there; this is not a safe place."

I made my way back to the theatre, my mind racing with questions. Who was the mystery person who had rescued me? And what connection did they have to the theatre and Lily White's ghostly presence? As I approached the Majestic's front entrance, I noticed a figure standing in the shadows. My heart raced as I recognized Sam's shadowy image.

"What are you doing here?" I demanded, my voice laced with suspicion. "I've been looking for you."

He replied, his eyes darting nervously.

"When we were separated at the warehouse, and after you didn't return to the theatre, I became worried. I knew something was wrong. You know, Mr. Foley, I did warn you about digging into things that are none of your business."

I studied his face, searching for any signs of deceit.

"I headed back to the theatre to look for Bill," he continued. “Are you ok? You look disheveled, and there's blood on your neck."

I hesitated, unsure of how much to reveal. "There's more to this place than meets the eye," I said cautiously. "I believe Lily White's spirit is trying to communicate something, and someone doesn't want that information to come to light."

Sam swells his chest, brow furrowed, and steps closer, his voice lowering,

"I found Bill, he’s inside waiting for you.”

Still feeling the effects of the warehouse episode, I hesitantly follow Sam into the theatre. My eyes dart around each corner as we approach, never losing Sam in my sight. A mistake I will not make again.

We enter the theatre doors, Sam begins,

“I, too, have experienced strange phenomena and felt the presence of something otherworldly here. Bill was weak and grew weary of fighting for what our parents sacrificed everything for."

The air was thick and heavy. Breathing was almost a laboring task. The lights flickered, and the hum of electricity was distant and disturbing. Sam leads me into their office. He pushed open the heavy oak door, the hinges groaning a protest that echoed the unease tightening in my chest. His office was dimly lit; the only light came from a single desk lamp, casting a harsh circle on the cluttered mahogany surface.

Bill, Sam's partner, was slumped over his desk, his head resting awkwardly on a stack of papers. One hand dangled limply over the edge, a half-empty glass of amber liquid precariously close.

"He was about to call the authorities again." Sam's voice was low and emotionless. The words hung in the air, heavy and sharp. "He was ready to turn us in. I... we had to stop him."

I stared at Bill, the stillness of his form unsettling. My mind raced. Had Sam actually stopped him? Or...? The implication hung between us, an unspoken accusation. I swallowed; the dryness in my throat was a reflection of the uncertainty in my gut.

My eyes scanned the room, landing on a small, intricately carved wooden box nestled amongst the scattered paperwork. It looked out of place, almost deliberately hidden. A detail that shouldn't have caught my eye, yet it did. It felt significant somehow, a clue that hadn't been there just moments before. I couldn't shake the feeling that this was more complicated than Sam's explanation suggested.

“Perhaps Bill hadn't been ready to betray you at all. Perhaps... something else had happened.” I began, my voice a mere breath. The question was more than just about the method; it was about the motive.

“Why would Bill, your longtime partner, suddenly decide to turn against you?”

Sam sighed, running a hand through his already disheveled dark hair.

"It was...or is complicated. Let's say he had a change of heart. A rather... forceful one."

He didn't elaborate, his gaze distant and unsettlingly calm. The silence that followed was thick with unspoken questions and unanswered anxieties.

My gaze locked onto Bill, the co-owner of the theatre. An icy dread gripped me; his motionless body surpassed mere unconsciousness. It felt calculated, a performance of unsettling stillness, almost cruelly staged. My eye caught a hint of movement in my periphery. My attention was drawn from Bill's lifeless body to a small, almost imperceptible shift in the shadows through the window. A dark shape, too swift to be defined. My heart pounded. I was certain I'd seen something, something that defied explanation.

"Sam," my voice was shaky and urgent, "We should go." My focus shifted away from Bill, toward the window and the unseen presence that had just given me a profound sense of unease. The wooden box, the amber glass of liquid, and Bill's lifeless body all remained fixed in my mind. There was more to this, and I had a growing suspicion that it was far, far worse than a simple betrayal.

I turned to leave; the mahogany door handle was cool beneath my fingertips. Then a metallic glint caught my eye. Sam's hand, previously hidden behind his back, now held a pistol. He leveled it at me.

"I can't let you ruin everything," his voice surprisingly calm, a stark contrast to the lethal object in his grip. "Bill tried, and you, you are not going to succeed either."

My heart pounded a frantic rhythm. Sam moved closer, his hand shaking from the gravity of this inescapable situation. His voice became distant and garbled. I felt he was not really talking to me; he was talking to someone or something else.

“This wasn't how it was supposed to end. This wasn't supposed to happen at all. He was a good man, he was family, even. Or so I thought. The years we'd shared, the laughter, the mutual support, all dissolving in the cold, hard certainty of this moment.”

The gun looked unreal, a prop in some badly written play. He pressed the barrel into my ribs. I felt the cold, hard steel through my thin shirt. His almost inhuman voice said,

“Over here, sit across the desk from Bill.” He gestures with the gun, pointing in the direction of his once partner. Without thinking, I swiftly turned and grabbed the gun; we grappled, almost falling over Bill. A brutal, silent struggle for control of the weapon. It was heavier than I expected, the cold steel biting into my skin. His grip was surprisingly strong, desperate. I felt a surge of adrenaline, pure, raw fight-or-flight. The scent of gun oil and something acrid, fear perhaps, or sweat filled the air.

"This isn't right, Sam," I managed to gasp out, my voice barely a whisper against the thunder of my pounding heart. "We can still fix this."

"No," he growled, his eyes wild. "It's too late." Then, a deafening crack. The gun discharged. The world seemed to tilt on its axis, the sound echoing in the sudden, suffocating silence that followed. The gun clattered to the polished wooden floor. We separated, gasping for breath, our bodies trembling. He stumbled back, clutching at his chest. A crimson stain bloomed slowly on his white shirt, spreading like an ominous flower. I stared, frozen. A single, horrible thought dominated my mind: Did I cause this?

"I didn't mean to. It wasn't supposed to go off like that. I...I didn't..." He said, his voice barely audible, the words trailing off into a shaky sigh. Blood continued its slow, relentless descent. The silence returned, broken only by the sound of my ragged breathing, a counterpoint to the gurgling, rasping breaths escaping his lips.

The air was thick with the smell of blood and the lingering scent of fear. The unexpected consequence of a misguided loyalty, a desperate attempt to salvage something now utterly shattered. The gun lay now harmless on the floor, a cold, metallic testament to the unraveling of everything I thought I knew. The ornate details of the room, the expensive Persian rug, the antique furniture, all seemed to blur, their luxury grotesquely compared with the reality of the dying man before me. He looked up at me, his eyes already glazing over, and I saw nothing but the cold fear and regret of a dying man.

The silence was deafening. Dazed, confused, and disoriented, I picked up the phone and dialed Detective Johnson's number on the card he had given me.

"Detective, this is DB. I'm at the theatre. Can you come over here? Something has happened."

Chapter 6

The Steel Staircase

I was taken aback by a loud bang on the theatre's outer doors. A large-bodied man breached the entrance, storming into the lobby with his gun drawn. A rush of relief enveloped me as I recognized Detective Johnson.

A thick metallic reek filled the air, the scent of blood a stark contrast to the faint, sweet perfume still clinging to it. Bill lay across his desk, cold and rigid, with a pale grey complexion, his eyes wide and vacant. The glass of golden liquid, now, spilled from the struggle between Sam and me, soaking the paperwork beneath his head. Sam was sprawled across the ornate Persian rug, a bright red stain blossoming on his white dress shirt.

Detective Johnson knelt beside them, his practiced gaze already assessing the scene. I swallowed, the dryness in my throat making the words difficult.

"It... there was a struggle," I began, my voice trembling slightly despite my efforts at composure. "Sam and I... we fought for the gun. It went off. He... he was hit." I gestured vaguely at Sam's chest.

The detective didn't react, his expression unchanging.

"And Mr. Bill?" he asked, his voice low and measured.

"He... he was already dead when I arrived. I think... I think he'd been drugged." The last part felt like a whisper, lost in the sudden, unsettling silence. A silence broken only by the rhythmic beating of my own heart, like a frantic drum. Then, it started. A soaring soprano voice, rich and clear, drifted from the main theatre. An aria, mournful yet strangely beautiful, filled the otherwise grim space with a dissonant yet captivating melody.

"What's that?" Johnson asked, his head tilted slightly. His eyes narrowed, no longer focusing solely on the bodies. There was something else he was processing. A subtle shift in his bearing suggested a different line of inquiry was forming in his mind.

"The theatre," I replied, my voice still a mere whisper. A strange unease coiled in my stomach. This wasn't just a simple murder; it felt orchestrated, theatrical even. This haunting melody enhances the chilling scene rather than masking it. He nodded, his gaze already leaving the corpses, drawn by the haunting melody.

“Let’s go take a look.” We moved towards the theatre, the music growing louder, more insistent. The air inside the theatre was thick with the smell of lavender and rose. The stage was empty, the curtain closed, the only light emanating from a single spotlight aimed directly at the orchestra pit, which was strangely empty, except for a single, antique gramophone, playing a worn vinyl record. The soprano voice seemed to emanate from the gramophone itself, somehow amplifying and manipulating the sound in a way that seemed almost impossible.

"This isn't live," Johnson muttered, his eyes fixed on the gramophone. "It's... a recording, and incredibly well done." He approached the machine cautiously, his hand hovering over the needle.

"But... the voice," I said, a shiver tracing its way down my spine. The uncanny realism and the emotional weight of the performance were unsettling. It was so close to reality. I watched the detective's hand hover over the gramophone; he switched it off, but the notes did not fall silent.

The smell of sweet perfume continued to fill the theatre as the red velvet main curtain opened slowly. The scene is set. The sound of music filled the room, and a soft, ethereal light appeared on the stage. We stood transfixed as a woman's figure emerged, dressed in a white gown. Her voice, like a haunting melody, filled the theatre.

"Welcome," she said, her eyes fixed on me.

"You are the one who can free my spirit. I plead with you to reveal the truth, and my spirit will be free."

I felt a rush of adrenaline as I realized the spirit of Lily White had returned.

"Why?" I asked, my voice shaking.

"Why me?"

Lily's gaze softened as she glided closer, her voice carrying a hint of sadness.

"Because only you have the power to set me free. Only then can this theatre truly be at peace."

Instantly, the spotlight found me awkwardly center stage, the velvet curtain a heavy, suffocating presence behind me. Lily's translucent form shimmered, barely visible, yet undeniably there. She was dressed as she had been in 1961, in a shimmering white gown, a stark contrast to the dusty, aged theatre around us. It felt surreal, like a dream that blurred the lines between reality and an impossible fantasy.

"The steel staircase," her voice, a whisper, cut through the silence.

"Beneath it, a hidden door. Within an envelope."

My heart was beating so fast I thought it would explode. Lily, a ghost, is directing me... to what? I'd always felt a strange connection to this old theatre, a pull I couldn't explain. Or was it something more... fantastical?

"The information you seek... It's there in plain sight," she continued, her ethereal form drifting closer.

"Bill and Sam's office. They never knew."

"But... why me?" I managed, my voice trembling slightly. I felt foolish, talking to a ghost, but the chill in the air was undeniable, the conviction in her voice impossible to ignore.

"Destiny," she replied, "It is destiny.

And the theatre... it needs you." She faded slightly, her form growing less defined, then more solid again, before dissipating entirely, leaving only the faintest trace of her sweet perfume in the haze of the soft light.

The stage felt colder now, somehow emptier. Taking a shaky breath, I found myself moving, propelled by a mixture of apprehension and a strange, almost desperate hope.

As I exited the stage, I found Detective Johnson watching intently from the shadows to my left. We navigated through the dimly lit backstage area, the air lingering with the scent of sweet perfume. My hope was that this was just a dream and I would wake in my office where a pile of contracts awaited my attention. This would not be the case.

Bill and Sam's office was impressive in size, their bodies still and cold where they had lain earlier that evening. I glance at the red stain of blood still glistening wet on Sam's white shirt. The steel spiral staircase is tucked away in the left corner. Sam's body, once filled with life, emotion, and vigor, now lay motionless, separating me from my destination. Stepping cautiously and deliberately, I step over his lifeless body. I make my way to the staircase. It wasn't merely a staircase; it was a monument to industrial design, with intricate, sculpted flowers painted black and cold.

Detective Johnson stares intently at their bodies, stone-faced and emotionless.

“I need to call this in.... In light of what I just witnessed, I can only give you 10 minutes, and then this place will be crawling with uniforms and detectives.” He walked to the lobby, and I could hear him on his phone.

I circled the steel staircase carefully, running my fingers along the cold steel. There was no visible door. A moment of panic. Was I imagining things? Was this some elaborate, theatrical hoax? Then, a faint click. A small, almost invisible lever was set into the base of the staircase, hidden beneath a layer of dust. I pulled it gently. A section of the wall beneath the staircase slid open, revealing a small, dark space. Inside, nestled amongst cobwebs, was a single, plain manila envelope. My hand trembled as I reached in and retrieved it.

My heart pounded as I slowly opened the envelope; inside was not a letter but a small, intricately cut key. It was old, its brass darkened with age, yet strangely warm to the touch.

There was no note, no explanation, just the key. A key to what? To Lily's past, maybe to the truth of Lily's death. Lily's ghostly whisper echoed in my mind, the enigmatic words "The theatre needs you" taking on a deeper, more urgent meaning. I had a feeling that this was only the beginning. This antique key, warm and strangely familiar, felt like the first piece of a puzzle spanning generations, a puzzle I was now compelled, and strangely, excited, to solve.

Detective Johnson interrupts my thoughts.

"If I had not been here to see what I saw, I would be hauling you off to the slammer. I believe there is more to this than we understand. What I saw on that stage can't be explained. Straighten your collar and compose yourself before the police dispatch arrives. Let me do the talking when they do."

Dispatch arrived at 12:47. The first two officers who entered the building stopped and talked with Detective Johnson.

Immediately, they made their way over to me, standing in the lobby just outside of Bill and

Sam's office, composed as best as I could. I found myself in a situation where no one wanted to find themselves.

"I'm Officer Davies. I need to place you in cuffs. You are not under arrest, just detained at this time."

He placed me in handcuffs and then escorted me to his police cruiser.

"Is this necessary, officer?" My mind was still on the envelope and key I found earlier. I needed to process everything in my mind. I needed to find the lock that the key belonged to before they did.

How long would I be detained?

What questions would I be forced to answer? Do I need a lawyer? So many questions ran through my mind.

The precinct was only a few blocks from the theatre. Nevertheless, the uncomfortable ride handcuffed in the back of a police cruiser seemed like an eternity.

The harsh fluorescent lights of the precinct office hummed, a counterpoint to the low murmur of voices from the adjacent briefing room. I sat across from two uniformed officers, Miller & Davies, their faces etched with the weariness of a long night. The air was filled with the scent of stale coffee and cigarette smoke.

“We need to take a full statement. If you can write down everything you can remember, starting from when you arrived at the theatre. Include your full name, address, and recent address for background information.”

The questioning continued for hours. At 9 am, Detective Johnson came in and sat adjacent to me, a man whose jowls seemed perpetually burdened by the weight of unsolved cases, leaned forward, his gaze intense.

"When I arrived at the Theatre," Johnson began, his voice a low rumble, "He, with a head nod toward me, wasn't on the scene yet."

Officer Miller responded, consulting his notepad.

“Our dispatch log indicates an arrival time of 00:47 hours. The crime scene processing continued throughout the rest of the night."

My interrogation was no different, as long as the night was dark. I asked, trying to keep my tone neutral, though a knot of frustration tightened in my stomach.

“Am I under arrest?”

Davis, with a half-restrained yawn, said,

“No, Johnson vouched for you, so we are releasing you. Don’t leave town and... make yourself available for further questioning if needed.”

My thoughts on the theatre, usually a beacon of vibrant life, now felt like a tomb in my memory, its cashmere rugs stained with something far more sinister than spilled wine.

“Can I go back to the theatre and gather my stuff?”

Officer Davies nodded.

"Yes, sir. We cleared around 6 AM. Extensive forensics, photography...the usual."

"The Usual," I repeated the words under my breath, the bitter taste of it clinging to my tongue. Nothing about last night felt usual. The meticulously placed clues, the almost theatrical arrangement of the body, it felt orchestrated, almost...performative.

Johnson tapped a pen against his thick file. I overheard him and Davies talking just outside the doorway.

"Anything unusual? Anything that stood out?"

"The victim's positioning was...odd," Miller said, his eyes flickering to Davies.

"Almost as if they'd been...posed."

"Posing wasn't my department's purview," Davies said stiffly. "But I will say the lighting was strange, even considering the state of the emergency."

"Strange lighting," I murmured, the image of the single, stark spotlight illuminating the body flashing in my mind. It was a detail that felt too precise, too deliberate, to be accidental. The theatre's sophisticated lighting system, normally capable of a thousand nuanced effects, was reduced to a single, harsh beam. Was it a deliberate choice by the killer? Or a malfunction? Or something else entirely?

"Did you notice anything unusual about the theatre itself?"

"Beyond the obvious?" Davies chuckled grimly.

"The place was not a mess, and there were no signs of forced entry. Surprisingly tidy for a crime scene, actually. That tidiness was what truly unnerved me. It wasn't the chaotic sprawl of a struggle. It was a calculated precision, a disturbing order imposed on the chaos of death. The killer hadn't just taken two lives; they'd staged a performance. And I'm certain we missed something vital, a piece of this morbid puzzle that would unlock the whole, terrible truth. A piece hidden perhaps, in plain sight."

"Thank you, officers," Johnson said, dismissing them with a curt nod.

As they left, I felt the pressure of the unanswered questions intensify. The theatre wasn't just a crime scene; it was a meticulously crafted stage. One question: who was the playwright of this tragic drama? Leaving behind a performance that would haunt my nightmares.

On the drive back to the theatre, I decided I would confront whatever secrets this theatre holds." As I entered the theatre, the familiar scent of sweet perfume filled the air again. I felt a chill run down my spine as I made my way back to the office. The room was dark and silent, but I sensed a presence lurking in the shadows.

"I can feel your presence," I whispered, my heart pounding, my eyes widening. It was as if someone was watching me. I made my way back to the steel staircase and found the hidden compartment at its base. A gentle push and the small door opened.

The aged Manila envelope felt brittle in my hands. I'd found it precisely where I left it, amidst cobwebs. I retrieved the tarnished key, its edges still crisp as if it had never been turned in a lock. I sat down studying the intricately cut key. I repeated Lily's words. "The information you seek... it's there in plain sight," "it's there in plain sight," "it's...there...in...plain...sight". My senses peaked, my eyes wide, I scanned every inch of the room. My heart flutters and skips a beat as I realize I am sitting at the very desk that Bill was slumped over merely hours earlier.

"In plain sight," exhausted with thought, I lay my head on the desk, eerily close to the same place I found Bill. I began to recognize that familiar smell of sweet perfume filling the heavy office air. With one swift movement, I raised my head. Directly in front of me, a soft, glowing beam illuminates the ornately crafted box on Bill's desk.

"In Plain Sight." I nervously held the tarnished key. A heavy silence fell over the room as I inserted it into the lock and slowly turned it counterclockwise.

Chapter 7

The Letter

The click of the lock opening was cathartic. The box opened, soft music and the sweet smell of lavender & rose emanated as the lid slowly hinged open. Several things were inside. I removed them one at a time. A contract, a bible, a bill of sale, and three photos. I debated myself about calling Detective Johnson. I decided to filter through the evidence first.

The photos intrigued me most; the old ones were yellow with age and a little ragged at the corners. I study them, but no one seems familiar. I lay them to the side. Next, I picked up the Bible, which reminded me of the family Bibles used in the early days, when the entire family would gather in the evening, and the head of the family would read from it before bedtime. I lay it beside the old photos. The names, signatures, and dates are all eerily familiar as I look through the old contracts. Samuel Bennett, Lily Bennett, William Hamilton, and Margaret London. On November 10, 1961, the contract is dated only 10 days before Lily White's accidental death.

The contract has to be the key to solving this puzzle. I read intently, studying each line carefully. It is filled with so much legal jargon, wherefores, and whereas you need a law degree to understand. Nevertheless, I continued reading, trying to understand what was involved and why the contract was written. Page three of the contract is the most interesting. It lays out a structure for the theatre's ownership. A trust from these four people was set up to ensure the finances would sustain operations for years to come. Ownership would pass to their heirs along with the money needed to operate the theatre. Mixed in the contract as I flip through the endless pages, a handwritten letter falls onto the desk. The beautiful handwriting stands out on the yellowing page.

It begins:

My Dearest William, My mind tells me everything about this is wrong. My heart tells a different story. When we met as young actors auditioning for our first play, I had no idea I would fall in love so deeply and quickly. Words feel inadequate to express the joy, the fear, and the profound sense of responsibility that fills my heart right now. I have something to tell you, something that will irrevocably change our lives, and I tremble at the thought of facing this unknown future without you. I am expecting, and I know this is not in your life plan. We were so very careful. I know this news carries a whirlwind of emotions, and I understand you will need time to process it. Please know that I will be leaving after tonight's performance. We both know the situation we have put ourselves in will not be a good one to raise and love an illegitimate child. St. Francis Home *for* Unwed Mothers *has arranged to handle everything very discreetly. I will be leaving on September 15. No one will need to know the details, and your dignity and standing in the town will remain secure. I have decided to place our child up for adoption and face whatever challenges lie ahead alone. I am not asking anything from you, just your understanding and space to heal from a mistake we cannot compound by bringing a newborn into our world of disarray. I will remember 1960 as one of my greatest failures as a mother. This news is a testament to the love we once shared, the passion that ignites our souls. But it also brings with it a weight of responsibility, a future I must now forge alone. I am scared, but I am also hopeful. I believe my love for this unborn child is strong enough to let it go to ensure a better life for him or her. One filled with love and promise of a future in a new direction, a new destiny.*

I am not sure what the future may hold or how we will navigate this new chapter. I do know that I once loved you more than life itself, but we cannot share this journey together.

With all my love, Lily

I decided to call Detective Johnson. My discovery of the letter and the contract, and their connection to the theatre's history, was too significant to ignore. As I dialed his number, my mind raced with questions. Who were these people mentioned in the contract? And how did they relate to Lily White and the theatre's hidden past?

"Detective Johnson," a familiar gruff voice answered.

"Hello, Detective, it's.... " I started, but he cut me off.

"I know who this is. What can I do for you, Foley?"

His tone was impatient, as if he were dealing with yet another nuisance call. I took a deep breath, steeling myself for what was to follow.

"I've made a discovery that might be relevant to your investigation. It's about the theatre's history and a contract dating back to 1961." There was a moment of silence, and then he said,

"Go on."

"I found a contract that establishes a trust between two families: the Bennetts and Hamiltons. It appears their heirs were to inherit the theatre and the finances to sustain its operations. The date on the contract is only ten days before Lily White's accidental death."

"Interesting," he murmured. "And you think this is connected to the recent events at the theatre?"

"I'm not sure, but it could be. The contract mentions Bob Bennett, Lily Bennett, Bill Hamilton, and Margaret London. Those names ring a bell, don't they?"

Another pause, followed by, "Yes, they do. We've been looking into the theatre's history and the people involved. This could be a missing piece of the puzzle. Can you bring the contract to the station?"

"Of course," I replied, relieved that he was taking me seriously. "I'll be there soon."

As I hung up the phone, my heart pounded with uncertainty. I felt like I was getting closer to the truth, but I also knew that the more I uncovered, the more dangerous my situation became.

The theatre's secrets ran deep, and Sam was willing to kill to keep them buried. I quickly gathered the contract and the other items. I had found the photos, the bible, and the bill of sale. As I examined them again, I noticed something strange. One of the photos showed a woman who resembled Margaret, the former performer I had met. Could it be her? And if so, what was her connection to all of this? With a sense of urgency, I made my way to the police station, my mind racing with questions and theories. I knew Detective Johnson and his team would uncover the truth behind the theatre's hidden history and the mysterious figures involved. But would they be able to do it in time to prevent another tragedy?

Consumed by anxieties over Lily White, the contract, and the letter, I drove to the precinct. I was undecided whether to reveal Lily White's most interesting letter to Detective Johnson, a concern I would be forced to confront. Upon entering the station, a whirlwind of frenetic energy engulfed every workspace. My gaze, sharp and apprehensive, scanned the room, searching for Johnson. As I paused near the entrance, an officer's concerned inquiry interrupted my hunt.

“Can I help you?”

"Detective Johnson, please," I replied. He gestured down the corridor, indicating the third door on the right; a path I now had second thoughts about taking.

The door was open, and I stood there patiently as Detective Johnson was on the phone. His gruff voice,

“I must speak with him as soon as possible. Have him call me when he gets in.”

He marks a notepad, closes it, and looks up at me,

“Okay, what is this about finding something relevant to my investigation?”

I laid the things I brought on the detective's desk: the photos, the Bible, and the contract. I hesitated as I thought about the letter. With a stern face and his brow raised.

"Is this everything you found? Where did you find it? My officers went through that place with a fine-tooth comb."

I turned and shut the door to prevent prying ears from hearing. With a whisper,

"I followed Lily's directions and found the hidden compartment behind the steel staircase. Inside, I found an envelope containing a key. The key opened the box, the box on Bill's desk. In the box, I found all of this."

The detective murmurs under his breath,

"So now we have ghost solving our cases." He looks me directly in the eyes,

"I'm not sure what I saw that night at the theatre, and I'm not so sure it wasn't an elaborate production put on just for a one-member audience, me. I don't think you are being forthcoming with everything you know."

As stern as I dared, to be standing in police headquarters, I leaned in toward Johnson,

"Detective, I have been nothing but honest and forthcoming, believe me, what happened at the theatre may have been surreal, but Lily was there."

Leaning back into his worn office chair, his arms crossed, he spoke in a low, controlled voice:

"I'm not speaking of the other night at the theatre, I'm speaking of your background. We have been investigating all aspects of this case. I personally have been digging into yours."

I tried to remain stone-faced, but my emotions got the better of me. My eyes told the story.

"What do you mean? I told Officer Miller and Davies everything about myself. I'm sure they checked it all out. Ask them, they will tell you."

"They did tell me, but you only told my officers half-truths. You told them you were born in South Carolina, moved to Florida, and then here. What you failed to tell them is you were adopted."

Detective Johnson's words were heavy, and accusatory. My heart dropped.

"Adopted? They have made a mistake."

"No, they assured me they have not. They followed the evidence, and it led to you today."

The idea felt like a physical blow, a total shift in the foundation of my life. Everything I believed, every memory, every carefully constructed family narrative, crumbled. South Carolina. Mill workers. Mom and Dad. Those words begin to sound foreign.

"Adopted, I was not adopted. My parents were mill workers from South Carolina. They are both deceased." My voice, I realized, was strangely steady, a thin veneer over the churning panic within.

"I need to do more research," Detective Johnson interjected, his tone more measured than my own.

"But so far I have found... in 1960, your mother worked at St. Francis Home for Unwed Mothers."

The room tilted. I took a deep breath. St. Francis. The name echoed in my mind, a chilling revelation. The same place in Lily's letter.

"It's a place where young women, ostracized and alone, gave birth in secret. A place where babies were... placed."

He paused, and I could see the wheels turning behind his eyes. A subtle shift in his posture made me feel uneasy.

"This is not an accusation, but simply a part of our investigation," his words gentler than I deserved, or more accurately, more gentle than I expected.

A wave of nausea washed over me. This wasn't just about the red truck that had almost killed me, the anonymous menace that haunted my dreams. This was about my entire identity, the very core of my being. My carefully constructed past disintegrated before me. At this point, I asked,

"Am I free to go?"

I managed, my voice barely a whisper. The words felt inadequate, empty gestures in the face of this overwhelming discovery. I wasn't free. I was adrift.

Detective Johnson showed no emotion, only a professional resolve and an air of grim determination.

"Yes, of course, you are not being detained."

The weight of his words felt heavier than the walls of the interrogation room. Outside, the city lights blurred through the rain-streaked window. The rain mirrored the storm raging inside me. I needed answers. Answers about the family I believed I had, the parents who were not my parents. And most urgently, I needed to find the man in the red truck. The same red truck that tried to run me over, the truck that had become a symbol of a much larger, more terrifying mystery now unfolding.

The image of the truck's taillights, two crimson eyes burning into the darkness, flooded my mind again. The truth, it seemed, was far more complex, far more terrifying, than I could have ever imagined. My past, once a familiar comfort, was now a maze of secrets and shadows. And I was alone, utterly alone, in its unsettling depths.

The investigation had uncovered a horrific, heart-wrenching fact. This was not the answer I was looking for. The rest of the night, I walked the streets of our small town, looking, hoping by some strange coincidence I would see the red truck.

The sleepless night was long; at some point, I found myself at the theatre. Wondering the halls seeking answers to both my own past and Lily's. Looking for something, anything that would shed light on the past or even my future.

I found myself sitting in my old office, sleepy and dazed, my head on my desk. Soft music begins, and a beautiful soft voice starts to sing. The smell of that familiar sweet perfume fills the office. This strangely renewed my vigor. I rose to my feet and made my way to the stage door. Lily is there in her beautiful white dress. She turns and motions to me,

"Come closer."

I walk out onto the stage. Lily begins,

"I only have a short time left. My spirit grows weaker each time I appear. It's only a matter of time, and my spirit will be lost and forgotten forever. Your family can fill in the missing pieces of your past in time. My destiny cannot be of my own making or by my own means. I may have gone too far as it is. You are the only one who can set me free and save the theatre and all of its memories."

With that, Lily fades along with the music and the perfume I have grown so accustomed to. I know time is imperative for Lily and her legacy.

Now I am torn: Lily needs me to help set her spirit on the right path, but now my thoughts are a blur, consumed with who I am and why I was abandoned as a baby. I desperately need to find my own path and history.

Chapter 8

Aunt Sara

The full weight of the situation had not sunk in. With Sam and Bill's passing, I wondered what would become of the grand old theatre. Over Christmas break, there were no shows or events scheduled for two weeks. This gave a little breathing room before a decision had to be made.

Early on the morning before the theatre was scheduled to reopen, the emotional tone of the day was set when I woke from a dead sleep to my phone ringing on the nightstand beside my bed. Rubbing my eyes and with an uncontrollable yawn, I said

"Hello."

The voice on the other end seemed cold and sterile.

"Hello, this is Mr. Smith with Simon and Felter. In the interest of the estates of Bennett and Hamilton, I have been authorized by the board of directors to offer you a job handling the day-to-day operations of the theatre. You have until 4 pm today to respond."

Knowing the gravity of Lily's predicament, the need to be close to all of the clues, and the love and pull I feel for this old theatre, I accepted the position on an interim basis. This will give me time to solve this elusive dilemma for Lily. I decided I would try to do both, set Lily free, and find my way.

In the days that followed, I reached out to my mother's sister, Aunt Sara, who lived in South Carolina, just a 30-minute drive from me. I made the short trip and spent the entire day with her. It had been a couple of weeks since my mother's funeral on January 10th, since I had last seen her. We settled in, eager to bridge the gap of the preceding years. Our conversation meandered through my childhood, touching upon the profound affection my parents harbored for me as an infant.

As our reminiscences unfolded, a sense of anticipation built in the atmosphere. While Aunt Sara fondly recalled moments from my younger years, my thoughts were drawn to the period just before and during my birth. The weight of unspoken words pressed upon me. At last, unable to contain my growing curiosity any longer, I blurted out the question that had been consuming me:

"Aunt Sara, was I adopted?"

A wave of stillness washed over her. Her gaze met mine, her hands gently enveloping mine.

"Your mother desperately yearned to share the complete story with you," she began, her voice laced with sorrow.

"She simply couldn't muster the courage. Then, her death came so swiftly. I understood her deep desire to confide in you, and I am so profoundly sorry that she is no longer here to reveal it in the manner she had envisioned."

Aunt Sara went to the hall closet and brought back a small metal box with a lock. She handed me the key and said,

"Everything you need to know is in this box."

With excitement and apprehension, I turned the key, removed the lock, and opened the box.

Inside, I found a contract. The name on it was Margaret London. My grandmother's name was Margaret. Margaret Ann Davies. The middle name, Ann, piqued my curiosity. My mom's name was Ann. My mother only gave general family information, never anything specific. The contract detailed a complex real estate transaction that was fifteen years prior. The other party involved was listed simply as Bennett Holdings. A familiar surname, Bennett. My adoptive mother once mentioned a man she called your uncle Bennett. A man I only met once at my mom's funeral. I ask Aunt Sara,

"Did he have a son? Could his name be Sam?

I pulled out my phone and searched online. Samuel Bennett. My eyes widened.

Samuel Bennett, CEO of Bennett Holdings. A photo appeared, a man in his late eighties, bearing a striking resemblance to Sam. The resemblance wasn't familial in the way I'd recognize in most fathers and sons. It was deeper, a shared skeletal structure, a certain set to the jaw, a strange, unsettling sense of despair hit me.

"This is Sam's father," I muttered to myself.

"I had no idea."

"Aunt Sara, you have been a tremendous help. Thank you for sharing, and I'll call again soon. I need to go."

The next day, I called the number Aunt Sara gave me. The name above the number was Bennett. I began, my voice measured and devoid of emotion despite the turmoil brewing inside.

"I'm sure you do not know me, but Aunt Sara gave me your number and said you may be able to clear up several questions I have about my parents."

The voice on the other end was anything but kind.

"She said you would be calling."

"Well, I found something... unusual. A contract with Margaret London's name on it. The other party is Bennett Holdings." There was a long pause.

"Margaret London...? That's... peculiar." His voice was taut.

"That name doesn't mean anything to me,"

I pressed.

"I thought it might be a relative of yours?"

He huffed.

"It's a complicated story."

"Complicated how?"

"First and foremost, I do know you, or of you I might say.

I stood there, phone in my hand, waiting to hear more, but nothing came. Despite the flood of facts, many unanswered questions lingered, questions I suspected would remain unanswered.

"I have just a few more questions."

Abruptly, he interrupts me, "No more questions."

The phone went silent, and the weight of not having answers weighed heavily on me. The contract, a seemingly innocuous piece of paper, had unraveled a carefully constructed family secret, replacing assumptions with a confusing new reality. It wasn't just a legal document; it was a roadmap to the past. I never knew existed, connecting a few dots I previously never imagined. The ornate wooden box, with its secrets and forgotten contents, had revealed more than just old papers; it had unearthed a secret history.

I searched the paperwork for Bennett Holdings' address. Hidden deep in legalese, I find a P.O. box, 641.

For the next few days, I hung out at the post office. I parked my car so I could see the edge of box 641 through the side entrance window. Between the second and third bite of the bagel I was having for breakfast, I looked up and saw someone inserting a key and opening box 641. My heart raced, I scrambled for the ignition, started my car, and slumped down in the seat.

I peered over the dashboard and watched as the elderly gentleman walked out and turned the corner just out of sight. I slammed the car into drive and pulled forward to see around the corner. I almost jumped out of my skin as I watched him open the driver's side door and enter the old red truck. The grey-haired, distinguished-looking gentleman sped away.

Like a detective in a crime novel, I followed the old red truck. It led me to a large estate just North of town. He pulled into a covered garage, and the door closed behind him. I jotted down the address and drove on.

Was this pursuit the right thing? Was I stepping onto a path from which there was no return? Not sure what to do with this new information, I drove back to the theatre. Without thinking, I parked in the back parking lot and entered backstage, just as I had for the last year. The familiar scent of the theatre usually brought comfort, but now it felt suffocating.

I needed a plan to expose what really happened that night, but the urgency warred with a creeping fear that I was chasing ghosts, that my obsession with Lily's death was blinding me. I needed something that would set Lily's spirit free and release her to her final resting place, a noble goal that felt diluted by my own desperate need for answers.

After hours of thinking, I believed I had a plan. It was reckless, demanding a level of deception I'd always hated. I will need help, and the only person I can think of or trust is Detective Johnson. But trusting him felt like betraying the justice I felt Lily deserved, a justice that demanded I handle this myself, however flawed that might be.

A couple of days had passed, and with the plan set in place, I made the trip to Samuel Bennet's house. The plan was to ask a few questions. Flesh out the information Mr. Bennett offered and see where it leads.

As I walked up the short sidewalk to the front door, my mind was a tangle of conflicting thoughts. I could feel the grip of fear tightening around my chest. I whispered,

“I think I’m walking into a trap.”

Yet, a stubborn defiance, fueled by Lily’s memory, pushed me forward.

I thought of all the mysterious things that happened over the last few months and years: Bill and Sam, the attack in the warehouse, the near miss with the red truck, and, of course, Lily's fall that ended her life. Each memory was a shard of glass in my conscience, reminding me of the danger and of the responsibility I felt to uncover the truth, even if it meant sacrificing my own peace of mind.

Before I knew it, I was knocking on the door. The same grey-haired man I had seen at the post office opened the door. His gruff voice was barely audible through the glass outer door, "Yes, what do you want?"

"Hi, I'm Sara's nephew. I called you the other day. If you have a few minutes, I have a few more questions.”

Agitated, he answered,

"I told you everything the other day. What more do you want?"

His hostility was a mirror to the uncertainty within me. Part of me wanted to flee, to abandon this dangerous pursuit. But another, darker part, the part that had grown emotionally exhausted and hardened by these events, urged me to press on, to confront him, to expose him.

I began, "There's a lot I do know, but there are gaps I think you can fill in."

He responded almost before I finished,

"I don't know anything more, and I don't think you do either."

He was lying, I could feel it, and the desperation to prove him wrong, to shatter his composure, was becoming overwhelming.

"What I do know is that you are Sam's father. You have tried to run me over several times in that red truck. And you were married to Lily. What I don't know is why you wanted to kill me."

The words tumbled out, with an anger I hadn't realized I possessed, an anger that felt alien and frightening. My words were pushing him, forcing a confrontation I wasn't sure I was ready for, one that might end with me as the victim, maybe the same as Bill.

He pushes the glass door open and grabs my arm,

“Come in, this is not something we need to be discussing on my front porch.”

He leads me down a hallway to what looks like the den.

He looked me in the eyes, and I could see the hate shine through. As we walk, his voice is shaky and uneasy.

"It's your fault; if you had not come along, we could have worked everything out."

His accusation landed like a physical blow, twisting the knife of self-doubt that had been embedded in my heart. Was he right? Had my interference, my pursuit of the truth, somehow triggered these horrific events?

"Your adoptive mother had kept a profound secret from you. She never disclosed the existence of your biological mother. Nor the fact that this woman bore a son out of wedlock.”

His words were filled with disgust, a disgust that seemed to echo the judgment I saw in his eyes. This man really hated me.

This revelation settled upon me, inducing a dizzying sensation. The image of my mother, that stern and guarded figure, fractured, replaced by the stark realization that she was not my mother at all.

This was a betrayal, so intense and unexpected, that it threatened to undo me. I had clung to the certainty of my identity, and now, that foundation had crumbled.

He blurted out,

"You are that son."

The truth, raw and brutal, and it hit me with the force of a physical blow. My mind reeled, struggling to reconcile the man standing before me, the man who had tried to kill me not once but twice. The desire to expose Lily's killer suddenly felt secondary to the overwhelming need to understand this monstrous twist of fate.

I had sought justice for Lily, but now I was drowning in a personal catastrophe, forced to confront a past that was more terrifying than I could have ever imagined.

The choice was stark. Pursue the truth about Lily, or grapple with the reality of my own fractured identity. And for the first time, I felt lost, paralyzed by the thought of what had just been revealed.

Searching for more answers, I asked,

"So, my birth mother, Lily, gave me up for adoption and just severed all ties?" I inquired, my voice barely audible, a twinge of something related to betrayal already humming beneath my skin.

"That's not precisely accurate," he clarified, his tone measured, each word a carefully placed stone on a path I was being forced to walk.

"There were extenuating circumstances. Legal actions. She insisted on maintaining some connection. A discreet, financially supportive arrangement, as that was the only avenue she perceived."

“Perceived.” I blurted out.

The word grated on me. Did she perceive me as a burden? A transaction? The idea warred with the first, fragile hope that perhaps she'd loved me and been forced to let me go.

"And my biological father?" I insisted, with desperation in my gut, wanting to anchor myself to at least one solid piece of this crumbling identity.

"That's where the situation becomes even more intricate. William and Lily, your birth parents, met and had an illicit love affair during their early acting careers, and you were the abomination of that union. As time passed, I was able to drive a wedge between them, and they grew resentful; their tempestuous relationship ultimately dissolved."

His head bowed slightly, and his voice softened.

"Lily was *my* wife."

The confession lingered, heavy and suffocating. I was the wedge. My existence was the cause of their downfall. My stomach twisted, and the very foundation of my being felt like quicksand. Had I, unknowingly, caused such pain? The man speaking, my mother's husband, had orchestrated this destruction. And I, the innocent child, was the weapon. A wave of nausea washed over me. Should I condemn him for this, or accept it as a part of the messy, complicated truth of my origin?

"Then Bill is her son, too?" The question felt both unavoidable and terrifying.

His head began vigorously shaking side to side

"No."

A weariness filled his response, as if he, too, was burdened by the weight of these truths.

"Bill's parents were Margaret and William. You and he are half-brothers; he's a year younger than you. They ought to have disclosed this to you after your adoptive mother's passing."

The finality of that statement, the casual dismissal of my adoptive mother's importance in revealing this, felt like another stab. My adoptive mother, who I grieved for, who had been my constant, my anchor, was apparently kept in the dark about this monumental piece of my heritage. A profound sense of guilt ate at me. Had she suspected? Had she suffered in silence?

My thoughts churned uncontrollably. This waterfall of information was overwhelming, far exceeding my capacity to comprehend. I was being handed pieces of a puzzle that didn't fit, forced to assemble a picture that was both alien and terrifying.

My entire life, the story I'd clung to, was a carefully constructed lie. And now, I was expected to accept this new, broken reality.

"I'm almost hesitant to ask, but how does Sam fit into this family tree, and why did he kill Bill?"

The words felt like I was wading through molasses, each inquiry another step further into a swamp of deception.

"Sam didn't kill Bill; I did. He was going to tell that detective everything. While you were at the warehouse, I had a final drink with Bill. I lined his glass with cyanide. I escaped out the side door in the office."

With an almost satisfying grin on his face.

"Sam was also your half-brother, but through your mother's lineage. Two years before you were born, Lily and I conceived a son. She blamed me, said I forced her into the relationship, and she was stuck in a loveless marriage. She was never going to accept him, and you took him from me."

Another brother. Another secret. Another piece of a life I didn't know I had, and one I now felt a perverse sense of obligation to claim, even as every fiber of my being screamed for escape. I felt a surge of anger so potent that it threatened to choke me. I wanted to scream, to lash out, but the sheer enormity of it all paralyzed me. My adoptive mother, the woman who had raised me, had held these secrets, had allowed me to believe so many falsehoods. Was it her duty to tell me, or mine to uncover? The choice between confronting her and burying this for the sake of peace was agonizing, a betrayal of my own quest for truth.

I stood there, staring out the picture window, shock, confusion, and intense disorientation filled my mind. My reflection in the glass seemed like a stranger's. I felt the urge to smash it, to shatter the existence of the devastating truth, but the knowledge, once exposed, could never be unlearned. I was left with the wreckage of my identity, forced to rebuild from the reality I hadn't known existed. A choice I never wanted to make, a failure to comprehend that left me unanchored.

I was caught off guard when I turned to confront Mr. Bennett, the cold metal glinting in the dim light. The large gun he held was pointed at my chest. With rage in his eyes, a rage that mirrored a dark, forbidden part of myself.

"Since you know most of my secrets, you may as well know them all. Lily didn't simply trip and fall; it was me. I intentionally left the rigging loose that night. When she pulled away from William and fell, she didn't have a chance.

You know, she planned to leave me and build a life with *that* man, once my best friend. Now that you know the full story, you have run out of chances as well."

My mind reeled. My birth mother. Was her death... my responsibility too? The guilt was a physical blow, stealing my breath. Nothing in life can prepare you for a situation like this. A gun six inches away from your chest, with the crushing weight of this new revelation reeling in my mind. I would have to accept this, to carry this burden to my grave.

My eyes remained fixed on the rather large gun in his hand. The hammer on the weapon began to move. A defining shot rang out. I gasped, and my eyes slammed shut. I grabbed my chest, expecting to feel the flow of my own warm blood. The release of this torment was a contrary thought that shocked me. But the expected pain, the finality, didn't come. Instead, I felt a jolt, a sickening thud. When I opened my eyes, Samuel Bennett was lying on the floor. A crimson stain expanding on his white shirt. To my right, Detective Johnson stood with his gun drawn.

My own hands were trembling, not just from fear, but from a horrifying realization. The moment I saw the gun aimed at me, the raw terror, the primal urge to self-preserve, had made me hesitate. And in that hesitation, in that desperate moment, I froze. My own mother's murderer was dead, and in a twisted way, I had caused it.

Out of the chaos, a calming voice asks, "Are you okay?"

My voice cracked with anxiety, a raw tremor that contradicted any sense of victory,

"You cut that pretty close, didn't you?"

“Did I cut it close? I had to wait until I was sure and he confessed everything."

His words, meant to reassure, only amplified my unease.

"Did you get everything you needed?" I asked, my voice barely a whisper.

"Yes, everything. The wire you wore worked perfectly."

I knew, with a chilling certainty, that this moment, this salvation, would haunt me forever. I had survived, but at what cost?"

The Final Curtain Call

Lily's Farewell

Returning to the theatre, I felt a revitalized determination. I began to settle into the recently renovated administrative spaces. A gentle melody drifted in, originating from the auditorium itself. Pushing open the grand entrance, I was enveloped by the delicate fragrance of perfume. A subtle light illuminated the stage's focal point. Across this space, Lily the Lady in White glided with an unhurried grace.

"Greetings, my son," she began, her voice a resonant whisper.

"I foresaw your triumph. Relinquishing you for adoption was never my desire, a truth I pray you now know. My profound affection for you was strong enough to give you the best chance to overcome the formidable challenges ahead.

This is my final manifestation before you. Understand that my love for you is eternal, and I shall forever remain by your side, a watchful guardian. Although my spirit has now found liberation, I leave you with this enduring token. Whenever your confidence falters, take a deep breath. The sweet smell of perfume shall serve as a testament to my perpetual presence."

The inexplicable pull towards the theatre was undeniably strong, a tangible link to my mother and an unforeseen familial heritage. I am now determined to carry on a legacy destined to endure through countless generations.

Assuming the position of Director, I began securing exceptional productions that would undoubtedly please Lily. That afternoon, Detective Johnson paid a visit and delivered the news of the official closure of all outstanding investigations into the Majestic, including the case involving Miss Lily White.

Ten weeks had passed. Ten weeks since Lily's vibrant presence had last graced the halls of the Majestic. Yet, on occasion, the sweet smell of lavender and rose would drift through the corridors, a fragrant whisper of a mother's enduring love, a testament to a connection that transcended even the veil of death.

A Diagram of our family tree.

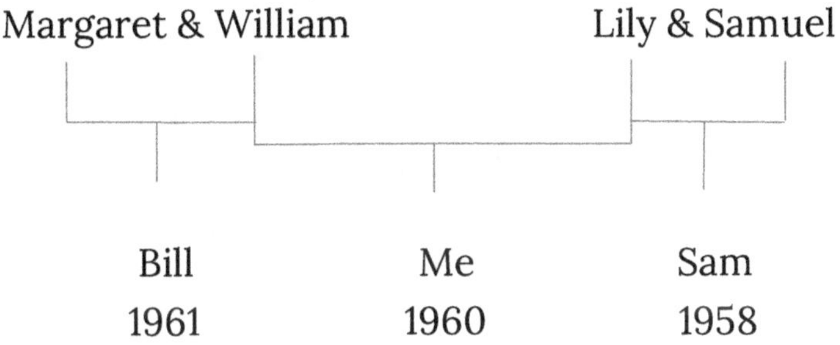

About the Author

As an artisan, I honed my pottery and woodworking skills independently, finding solace and fulfillment in creative pursuits during my leisure hours. My distinguished career as a journeyman tool and die maker provided a solid foundation, complemented by four decades immersed in the vibrant world of entertainment promotion. Capping this journey, I have served for the past fifteen years as the Executive Director of a thriving Art Deco theatre, originally built in 1939, where I book and present musical performances for large and enthusiastic audiences. Long days and nights were spent working, drinking coffee, and living the dream, and this book is a result of some of those long nights.

Acknowledgments

My deepest gratitude goes to my wife, family, and friends who sustained me through countless late nights and endless revisions. Ironically, a significant turning point in my life came while in a high school journalism class. My classmates suggested I abandon journalism and the writing courses and pursue other avenues after high school. It's a testament to the power of perseverance that, after 47 years, I've finally returned to this passion. This journey proves that the dreams of youth, however dormant, can blossom at any age.

Finally, and most profoundly, I owe an immeasurable debt to my mother, whose boundless belief in my potential and her consistent encouragement to embrace new challenges. Her unwavering belief in my capabilities instilled in me the courage to pursue my ambitions. Her words, "You can accomplish anything," echoed through the years, propelling me forward and fueling this improbable journey.

Thanks for reading! Please consider leaving a short review on Amazon, and let me know what you thought!

Other books by Stan Lowery: "The Coffee Shop Chronicles" and "A Theatre's Plea."
(From Dereliction to a Dream)
Find them on Amazon

I'll see you at the theatre!

www.ingramcontent.com/pod-product-compliance
Lightning Source LLC
LaVergne TN
LVHW010839120826
845149LV00017B/3317

* 9 7 9 8 9 9 4 6 0 9 2 1 7 *